Baby animals in land habitats

Bobbie Kalman

🌳 Crabtree Publishing Company
www.crabtreebooks.com

The Habitats of Baby Animals

Created by Bobbie Kalman

Dedicated by Dexter and Bonnie Crabtree
for Lilah Harvey Bradley
We love you!

Author and
Editor-in-Chief
Bobbie Kalman

Editors
Kathy Middleton
Crystal Sikkens

Design
Bobbie Kalman
Katherine Berti
Samantha Crabtree
(cover)

Photo research
Bobbie Kalman

Print and production coordinator
Katherine Berti

Prepress technician
Katherine Berti

Illustrations
Barbara Bedell: pages 15, 22 (ostrich)
Katherine Berti: page 22 (except ostrich)

Photographs
Corel: pages 13 (bottom), 18 (inset),
   24 (top right and left)
Digital Vision: page 19 (top right)
iStockphoto: pages 14 (left), 22, 24 (homes)
Photos.com: pages 14 (bottom), 23 (top)
Shutterstock: front and back covers and all other photographs
Wikipedia/NPS/John Good: pages 8
   (bottom left), 10 (bottom right)

Library and Archives Canada Cataloguing in Publication

Kalman, Bobbie, 1947-
   Baby animals in land habitats / Bobbie Kalman.

(The habitats of baby animals)
Includes index.
Issued also in electronic format.
ISBN 978-0-7787-7731-1 (bound).--ISBN 978-0-7787-7744-1 (pbk.)

   1. Animals--Infancy--Juvenile literature.
2. Habitat (Ecology)--Juvenile literature. I. Title.
II. Series: Kalman, Bobbie, 1947- . Habitats of baby animals

QL763.K343 2011   j591.3'9   C2011-902549-3

Library of Congress Cataloging-in-Publication Data

Kalman, Bobbie.
  Baby animals in land habitats / Bobbie Kalman.
     p. cm. -- (The habitats of baby animals)
  Includes index.
   ISBN 978-0-7787-7731-1 (reinforced library binding : alk. paper) --
   ISBN 978-0-7787-7744-1 (pbk. : alk. paper) -- ISBN 978-1-4271-9715-3
(electronic pdf)
   1. Animals--Infancy--Juvenile literature. 2. Animal ecology--Juvenile
literature. I. Title.
   QL763.K356 2012
   591.3'9--dc22
                                                    2011013879

Crabtree Publishing Company

www.crabtreebooks.com   1-800-387-7650

Printed in China/082011/TM20110511

Published in Canada
Crabtree Publishing
616 Welland Ave.
St. Catharines, Ontario
L2M 5V6

Published in the United States
Crabtree Publishing
PMB 59051
350 Fifth Avenue, 59th Floor
New York, New York 10118

Published in the United Kingdom
Crabtree Publishing
Maritime House
Basin Road North, Hove
BN41 1WR

Published in Australia
Crabtree Publishing
386 Mt. Alexander Rd.
Ascot Vale (Melbourne)
VIC 3032

What is in this book?

What is a habitat?

A **habitat** is a place in nature where plants and animals live. Plants and animals are **living things**. Living things grow, change, and make new living things. Plants make new plants, and animals make babies. This mother guanaco has a baby. She and her baby live on top of a **mountain**. Learn about mountain habitats on pages 20–21.

guanaco

Living and non-living

Habitats are made up of living things and **non-living things**. Air, sunshine, rocks, soil, and water are non-living things. Living things need non-living things. Plants need sunshine, air, and water to make food. They grow in soil. Animals also need air, water, and sunshine to stay alive. Plants and animals need other living things, too. Plants need animals to help them make new plants. Animals need to eat other living things to stay alive.

rocks

grasses

soil

bush

5

Land habitats

There are many kinds of habitats on land. **Forests**, **grasslands**, and **deserts** are some land habitats. Forests are habitats with many trees. Grasslands are flat areas that are covered mainly with grasses. Deserts are dry, sandy, or rocky areas that do not have a lot of trees. Some land areas are made up of several kinds of habitats.

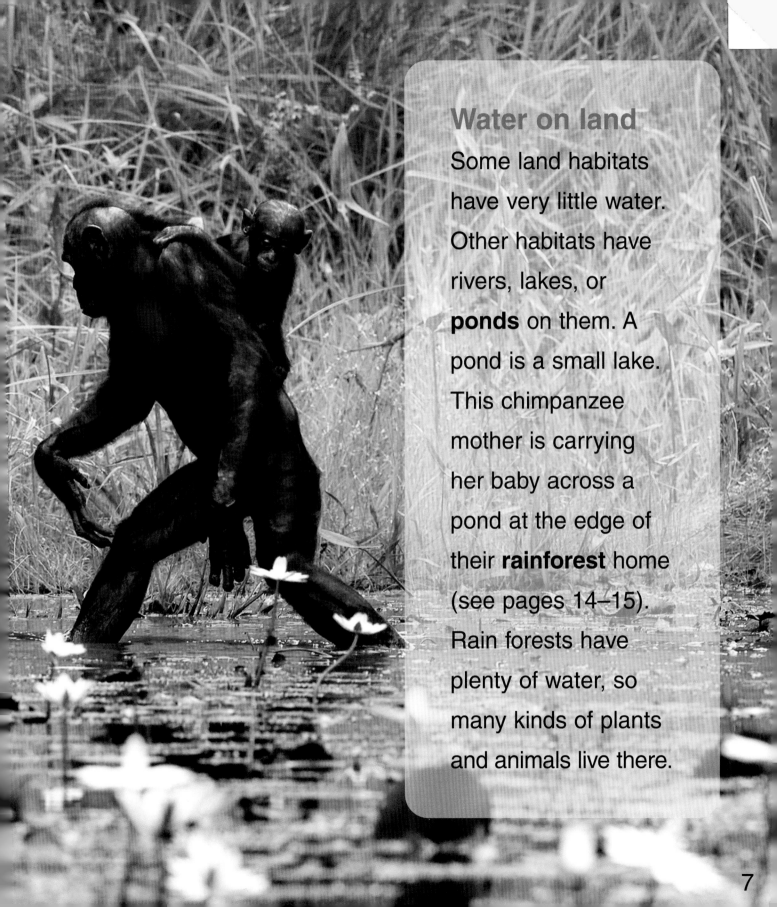

Water on land

Some land habitats have very little water. Other habitats have rivers, lakes, or **ponds** on them. A pond is a small lake. This chimpanzee mother is carrying her baby across a pond at the edge of their **rainforest** home (see pages 14–15). Rain forests have plenty of water, so many kinds of plants and animals live there.

Babies on land

baby chipmunk
*(most land
habitats)*

These are just a few of the baby animals that live in land habitats. Some have one main habitat, and others can be found in different habitats on several **continents**. Continents are big areas of land on Earth. Find the continents of some of these animals on a map or globe.

*red fox kit
(most land
habitats)*

*cougar cub
(most land
habitats)*

*wolf pup (some
land habitats)*

*coyote pup
(most habitats in
North America)*

*prairie dog pup
(prairie grasslands
in North America)*

*bobcat cub
(many habitats in
North America)*

baby
orangutan
(rain forests
in Asia)

mountain goat kid
(mountains in
North America)

baby sloth
(rain forests in
South America)

meerkat pup
(deserts
in Africa)

baby capuchin monkeys
(rain forests in Central America,
which is part of North America)

white rhinoceros calf
(savannas in Africa)

baby chimpanzee
(rain forests in Africa)

ostrich chick
(savannas
and deserts
in Africa)

baby guanaco
(mountains in
South America)

Food in habitats

baby
mouse
or rat

bird chicks

Animals that can live in different habitats have a better chance of finding food. You might even find them in your back yard! Mice and rats, chipmunks, deer, raccoons, rabbits, squirrels, coyotes, opossums, and many kinds of birds can live almost anywhere. Which of these baby animals have you seen in your back yard?

bunny rabbit

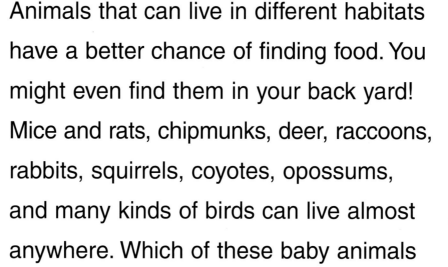

raccoon kit

baby chipmunks

baby squirrel

deer fawn

opossum joey

coyote pup

What is a food chain?

Animals need **energy**, or power, to breathe, move, grow, and stay alive. They get their energy from eating other living things. A **food chain** is the passing of energy from one living thing to another. When an animal eats a plant and another animal eats that animal, there is a food chain. The food chain on this page is made up of oak acorns, a chipmunk, and a red fox.

Plants make their own food from air, water, and sunlight. Using sunlight to make food is called **photosynthesis**.

An oak tree has made its own food. Its leaves and acorns contain some of the sun's energy.

acorns

red fox

chipmunk

When the chipmunk eats the acorns, it gets some of the sun's energy.

When the fox eats the chipmunk, some of the sun's energy is passed along from the acorns to the chipmunk and then to the fox.

Four-season forests

A forest is a habitat with many trees and other plants. Not all forests are the same. Some forests are in parts of the world where there are four **seasons**. The seasons are spring, summer, autumn, and winter. In each season, the temperature changes, and life is different for the baby animals that live there.

*These wolf pups were born in spring. Their mother keeps them safe in a **den**, or home, under a dead tree.*

In summer and autumn, baby animals learn to find food. This young bobcat has caught a chipmunk to eat. Bobcats are **carnivores**. Carnivores are meat eaters.

Winters are cold, and there is not as much sunlight. These baby cougars find less food to eat. Like bobcats, cougars are carnivores.

Rainforest babies

Some forests are in parts of the world where the weather is always hot. These forests are called **tropical forests**. In some tropical forests, it rains every day. These forests are called rain forests. Many kinds of animals live in rain forests. Some of them are shown on these pages.

baby orangutan

baby margay

The baby orangutan lives in a rain forest in Asia. The baby margay lives in the rain forests of Central and South America. Both animals find food up in the trees.

This capuchin monkey and her baby live high in rainforest trees.

This baby golden lion tamarin is part of a big family group in the rain forest.

baby green tree python

adult

This baby green tree python is yellow now, but it will be green as an adult.

baby sloth

This baby sloth hangs on to its mother. Sloths hang upside down in trees.

What are grasslands?

Grasslands are large, flat habitats that are covered mainly with grasses. Some grasslands have a few trees and **shrubs**, or bushes. There are grasslands in many parts of the world. Some are in places with four seasons. **Prairies** are large grasslands with four seasons.

These baby prairie dogs are coming out of their *burrow*, or underground home. It is their first time above ground.

What is a savanna?

A **savanna** is a large grassland in an area where the weather is hot all year. Instead of four seasons, savannas have a **wet season** and a **dry season**. In the dry season, it does not rain for months! Savanna animals include elephants, rhinoceroses, giraffes, lions, and cheetahs.

This white rhino calf lives in a savanna in Africa. It eats a lot of grass to keep its large body alive. Rhinos are **herbivores**. *Herbivores are animals that eat mainly plants.*

Baby desert animals

Deserts are areas that get less than ten inches (25 cm) of rain or snow a year. Some deserts are hot, and some are freezing cold. Deserts can be hot during the day and cold at night. Some deserts get rain for parts of the year. The Sonoran Desert in North America has two rainy seasons.

These kit fox babies live in the Sonoran Desert. There are more kinds of plants and animals in the Sonoran Desert than in any other desert. **Cacti** *are the most common plants. Their leaves look and feel like sharp needles. The green plant behind this picture is a cactus.*

bat-eared fox kit

fennec fox kit

red fox kit

Animals lose heat through their ears. Losing heat helps keep them cool. Big ears lose the most heat. The ears of foxes that live in hot deserts, such as bat-eared foxes, fennec foxes, and kit foxes (page 18), are bigger than the ears of red foxes, which live in cooler habitats.

Meerkats, also called suricates, live in the deserts of Africa. They live in big family groups of 20 to 30 animals. The family members help one another find food, keep safe, take care of the babies, and guard their homes from danger.

Mountain babies

Mountains are areas of rocky land that rise high above the ground. Most mountains have steep sides. Steep sides rise almost straight up from the ground. There are different habitats on mountains. Trees and other plants grow at the bottom of mountains. At the top of mountains are habitats called **alpine tundras**. There are no trees in alpine tundras because the weather is dry, cold, and windy.

This guanaco and her baby live in an alpine tundra habitat at the top of a mountain in South America.

This mother mountain goat and her two kids have no trouble climbing because their feet have **hoofs** with two toes. Hoofs are hard toes that help mountain animals grip rocks.

Red foxes live in many kinds of habitats, including mountains. This mother red fox keeps her kit safe in a den under some big rocks.

den

Animal mothers

Not all animal mothers take care of their babies, but most **mammal** mothers take care of their babies for a long time. Mammals are animals with hair or fur. They are born live. After their babies are born, mammal mothers feed them milk from their bodies. Many bird mothers, and some fathers, also take care of their babies.

These coyote pups are **nursing**, or drinking their mother's milk. They live in a mountain habitat. Their den is under this big rock.

den

Cat mothers carry their cubs by the **scruff**, or back, of their necks. This cougar mother is carrying her cub to a new den in their forest habitat. She moves her cubs often to keep them safe from **predators**. Predators are animals that hunt and eat other animals, especially babies.

This ostrich mother is taking her chicks to find food in the savanna. Ostriches are **omnivores**. They eat grasses and other plants, but they also eat small animals, such as insects, lizards, and mice.

Words to know and Index

babies
pages 4, 8–9, 10,
12, 13, 14–15, 16,
18–19, 20–21, 22, 23

deserts
pages 6, 9, 18–19

food
pages 5, 10–11,
13, 14, 19, 23
food chains
page 11

forests
pages 6, 7,
12–15, 23

grasslands
pages 6, 8, 16–17

den

homes (dens)
pages 7, 12, 16,
19, 21, 22, 23

Other index words
alpine tundras page 20
carnivores page 13
herbivores page 17
mothers pages 4, 7, 12,
15, 21, 22–23
omnivores page 23
photosynthesis page 11
plants pages 4, 5, 7, 11,
12, 17, 18, 20, 23
prairies pages 8, 16
rain forests pages 7,
9, 14–15
savannas pages 9,
17, 23
seasons pages 12–13,
16, 17, 18

living things
pages 4, 5, 11
(**non-living things**
page 5)

mountains
pages 4, 9,
20–21, 22